This Book Belongs to:

Name

Date

Minnie Saves the Day

BOOK 1

The Adventures of Minnie

Minnie Saves the Day

written and illustrated by
Melodye Benson Rosales

Little, Brown and Company
BOSTON   NEW YORK   LONDON

First Edition

Library of Congress Cataloging-in-Publication Data
Rosales, Melodye.
    Minnie Saves the Day / written and illustrated by Melodye Rosales.
— 1st ed.
    p.   cm. — (The adventures of Minnie ; bk. 1)
    Summary: Hester Merriweather's grandmother gives her a handmade rag doll that proves to be very special indeed. Includes historical background on Chicago's African-American community during the 1930s.
    ISBN 0-316-75605-9
    [1. Rag dolls — Fiction.   2. Dolls — Fiction.   3. Toys — Fiction.
4. Afro-Americans — Fiction.   5. Chicago (Ill.) — Fiction.]   I. Title.
II. Series: Rosales, Melodye. Adventures of Minne ; bk. 1.
PZ7.R7138Mi   2001   99-19896
[Fic] — dc21

10 9 8 7 6 5 4 3 2 1

NIL

Printed in Italy

Dedicated to all the "special" voices who passed on invaluable, undocumented oral history about the Black Belt (Bronzeville), Chicago, Illinois, in the 1920s, '30s, and '40s.

My dear friend, life long mentor, and aunt, Myrtle Vivian Benson Mallory, Board of Education, Los Angeles, California (1921–1999)

Nora (Benson) Tichenor, Chief Cook; Chicago, Illinois (1899–1991)

Arnold Theodore Benson, Chef, Chicago, Illinois (1891–1983)

My mother, Wini Rose Benson, professional dancer

My aunt, Hazel Mae (Benson) Jones, Administrator, Chicago Housing Authority

June Amelia (Johnson) Finch, Board of Education, Chicago, Illinois (1927–1999)

Gwendolyn King, Board of Education, Chicago, Illinois

Swersie (Turpin Dumetz) Norris, Board of Education, Chicago, Illinois

Etta Lee Morris, Homemaker

SPECIAL THANKS TO:

John G. Keller, Editor and Publisher — You are a rare jewel, always willing to keep an open mind. We have learned much from each other. You are not only my publisher, but my friend as well. Thank you.

Sheila Smallwood, Art Director — How refreshing it is to work with a creative person who is willing to stretch beyond the crop marks in order to ensure the highest level of quality. Thank you for keeping the old traditions of excellence in place.

Meet The Merriweathers

BRONZEVILLE 1933

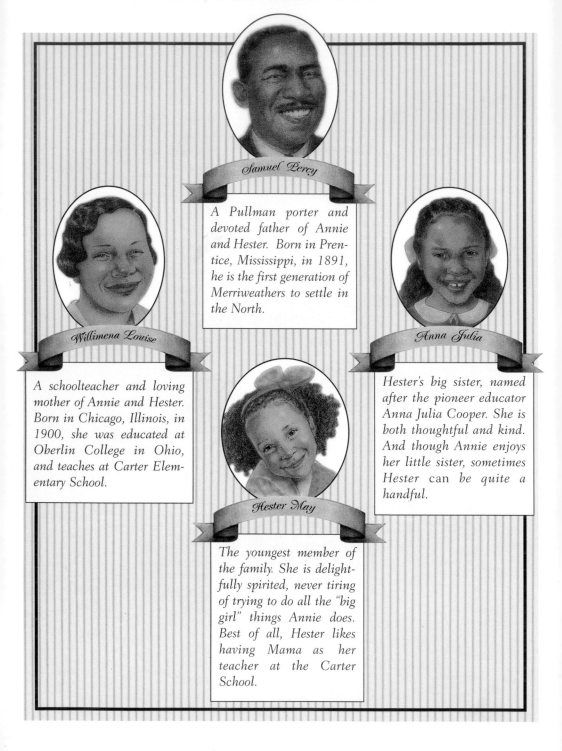

Samuel Percy

A Pullman porter and devoted father of Annie and Hester. Born in Prentice, Mississippi, in 1891, he is the first generation of Merriweathers to settle in the North.

Willimena Louise

A schoolteacher and loving mother of Annie and Hester. Born in Chicago, Illinois, in 1900, she was educated at Oberlin College in Ohio, and teaches at Carter Elementary School.

Anna Julia

Hester's big sister, named after the pioneer educator Anna Julia Cooper. She is both thoughtful and kind. And though Annie enjoys her little sister, sometimes Hester can be quite a handful.

Hester May

The youngest member of the family. She is delightfully spirited, never tiring of trying to do all the "big girl" things Annie does. Best of all, Hester likes having Mama as her teacher at the Carter School.

Contents

CHAPTER ONE

Grandmama's Gift

IT WAS A BRIGHT, summer afternoon, and Chicago's 12th Street Station was bustling with people, scurrying here, hurrying there, saying their hellos or their good-byes.

"Papa! Papa!" Hester called out as her father's face appeared through the crowd. She could always find Papa at the train station. He was a tall man who towered above most people. His dark brown skin and thick, black mustache gave his face a most handsome look. To Hester, Papa seemed like a king parading past his court as he gallantly strode down the wooden platform.

Since early morning, way before Sunday school, Hester Merriweather had been impatiently waiting for her father to arrive. Papa worked for the Illinois Central Railroad as a Pullman porter. Sometimes he would be away for days at a time, so Hester was always happy when he came home. But this time was even better. Papa was coming home after his trip down South. Hester knew that meant he was bringing her a

"Papa! Papa!" Hester called out as her father's face appeared through the crowd.

surprise from Grandmama Alfie, and she could hardly hold herself still.

"Papa! Papa!" Hester waved wildly back and forth.

Papa caught sight of Hester trying to stretch herself above the crowd. He gave her a wide smile and blew her a kiss.

Hester quickly climbed down from the station bench and tried to shove her way past Annie, her older sister, who was also there waiting with their mother.

"Stop pushing, Hester! Papa's got something for me, too, you know," Annie said.

Hester had barely slept a wink the night before. All she could do was imagine the big box with a pretty pink bow that Papa would bring the present home in.

But, as Papa came closer, Hester's excitement began to melt away. There was no big box in Papa's arms.

"What's the matter, puddin'?" Papa asked.

Hester's voice rose just above a whisper. "You forgot Grandmama's surprise."

"Oh, my!" Papa laughed. "Is that why you have those big ol' tears welling up in your little brown eyes?" Slowly Papa reached down into his large leather satchel and removed the soft, lumpy package Grandmama Alfie had carefully wrapped in brown paper and twine.

"Is this surprise enough to dry those weepy eyes?" Papa grinned as he handed the package to a happy Hester. Then he turned to Mama and Annie and gave them both a big hug.

"Papa," Annie said. "Isn't there something in your bag for me?"

Papa smiled. He pulled a small box from his coat pocket and opened it. Inside the box was a handmade bracelet crafted  from different-sized pebbles, no two of them alike. Each stone had been smoothly polished like glass and strung together with wire. A shiny brass heart delicately carved with tiny snapdragons sat in the center of the bracelet.

"Oh, Papa!" Annie cried. "It's so beautiful. I've never seen anything like it."

Annie eagerly held her arm out so Papa could fasten the bracelet around her wrist.

Mama and Hester took a seat on the station bench, and Hester excitedly tugged at the twine.

"I can help you if you like, Hester."

"I know how to do it, Mama. I can do it." Hester tore open the package. "*O-oh,* Mama! Look!"

There, beneath that plain brown paper, was the cutest little rag doll Hester had ever seen. Its soft, cotton body and face were an especially colorful toasty brown. And the mop

of dark yarn on top of its head was twisted into curls like water spouting from a fancy fountain. Sitting on top of that was a broad-brimmed hat. And covering the doll's red-and-white checkered smock, layered with a blue-striped pinafore, was a tightly knitted sweater. It had seven shiny buttons, each one with a look all its own. And peeking out from under the smock were white cotton pantaloons trimmed in lace. Each piece of clothing looked old and faded from years of wear.

Hester kept staring at the doll's face, gently touching its hair. She had never seen a colored doll before. Finally, Hester broke her trance. "Papa!" she called out as she held up the little rag doll for him to see. "Look! A doll! A pretty brown doll!"

"Ah, but that's not just any doll." Papa walked over to Hester. "Grandmama Alfie made her just for you. See —"

Papa pointed to a pink satin ribbon that was tied to the doll's left arm. At the end of the ribbon was a note:

> To my little Sugarpie,
> Now you have your very own
>   best friend. She's one of a kind,
>   so don't forget to give her a
>   "special" name.
> Love always,
>   your Grandmama Alfie

"Papa," Hester said, "nobody else in the whole wide world has a doll like this?"

"That's right, puddin'. Nobody. That's just one of the things that makes her so special."

"What's the other thing, Papa?" Hester promptly asked.

"Well . . . er . . . uh . . ." Papa hesitated, then cleared his throat. It seemed that he hadn't really thought of another special thing.

"Papa's saving that story for bedtime, Hester," Mama quickly chimed in. "Isn't that right, Papa?"

"Why, yes!" Papa said with relief.

"Oh, Papa!" Hester cried.

Then she reached out and squeezed her father with the biggest hug her arms could muster.

Hester gave Papa the biggest hug her arms could muster.

The family made their way to the car. Hester jumped in the backseat, snuggled close to the window with her doll, and whispered: *"Now we both can see where we're going, little doll."*

"Girls, I want you to write a nice letter to your grandmother and thank her for your gifts," Mama said.

"Yes, Mama," said Annie.

Hester didn't answer. She was much too busy whispering secrets to the little rag doll.

Mama was quiet as she climbed in the car and settled herself in the front seat. Papa knew that meant something was troubling her.

"How'd things go while I was away, Willie?" Papa said as he started the car.

Hester loved it when Papa called Mama, Willie. It was short for Willimena, and Hester thought it sounded warm and comfortable.

"Fine . . . I suppose." Mama turned her attention toward the window.

"What's troubling you?" Papa asked.

Mama turned back to Papa. "Well, it's just that my parents are coming for dinner tomorrow evening. You know they like everything to be just perfect, and I have so many things to do to get ready. Especially making that butter pound cake of mine — my father simply adores that cake."

"Just relax yourself, Willie. Everything's gonna be all right. Ain't no use worrying yourself about it now."

"Papa!" Annie exclaimed primly. "Mama always says, 'Don't say ain't because it's not in the dictionary.'"

"And I guess your Mama should know. After all, she *is* the best teacher at Carter School." Papa smiled and gave Mama a confident wink as they drove off, heading for home.

"Mama?" Hester gave a curious look at her doll. "Since my doll was born in Mississippi like Papa, does she talk like that, too?"

Everyone laughed, except Hester.

"That's silly, Hester," Annie said. "Dolls can't talk."

Hester turned back toward the window and whispered again to the little rag doll: *"You can so talk. I know it."*

CHAPTER TWO

A Friend Found

THE MERRIWEATHERS' home was on the South Side of Chicago, at 51st Street and Indiana Avenue, in a section known as Bronzeville. Their neighborhood sat right in the middle of the Black Belt, an area where many Negroes settled when they moved to Chicago from the South. It was 1933, the middle of the Great Depression and though jobs were scarce, Hester was lucky to have two working parents.

The family lived in one of thirty-two apartments in a large, three-story, brick courtway building, on the third floor. From their front window, Hester could look down into the courtyard at an oasis of grass and flowers, small trees and shrubs. Hester thought there was something grand about living in a courtway. She often went down into the courtyard to play different games of make-believe. Sometimes she would spread out a small blanket under the tree, with each toy in place. There beneath the shade they could all enjoy her delightful tea parties, with real soda crackers and sugar water.

A Friend Found

With each toy in place, they could all enjoy her delightful tea parties.

As Hester and her family walked toward their building, Annie ran ahead to meet a group of her friends who were gathered outside. As she approached them her best friend, Beatrice Johnson, called, "Annie Merriweather! We've been waiting for you all afternoon. The Billikens were supposed to have our club meeting after church today!"

"Sorry. Papa's train was late. As soon as I take these packages upstairs, I'll be right back." Annie dashed up to the family's apartment.

Mama came in behind her.

"Be back later, Mama," Annie said.

On her way back down the stairs, Annie brushed past Hester.

"Annie!" Hester tried to get her sister's attention. "Are we going to play today?"

"Oh, Hester. Maybe later," Annie answered, never stopping.

"Don't be late for supper, Annie!" Mama called down from the top of the stairs. "And don't get your Sunday clothes dirty!"

"Yes, Mama!" Annie said as she flung open the door to the courtyard.

When Hester reached the apartment, she hurried into the front room and climbed up on the straight-back chair in order to see Annie and her friends down below.

Annie proudly showed off her new bracelet to the group. All the girls wanted to try it on. Annie was the most popular girl in their neighborhood, and she was also president of the neighborhood's Bud Billiken Club, the most popular club for young Negroes in the Chicago area.

Lately, Annie always seemed too busy to play with Hester. Hester liked the way it used to be, when Annie had time to teach her new handclapping rhymes, take her roller-skating, and play hopscotch games. But now, when Annie was with her friends, Hester had to find her own things to do. Sometimes this made her feel lonely, like today.

"Hester," Mama said, breaking the silence. "Haven't I told you about climbing up on my good chair?"

"Yes, Mama," Hester replied.

Mama knew that Hester needed something to do. "Sweetheart, why don't you take your new doll to your room to meet your other toys? And as soon as I finish making my cake,

"Hester," Mama said. "Haven't I told you about climbing up on my good chair?"

I'll come in and read you a story. How's that?"

Hester had been so busy watching Annie that she had almost forgotten about her new rag doll. As Mama went back to her chores, Hester decided it was time to give her new doll the grand tour.

—◦◦◦◦—

Sweet smells of browned butter and vanilla lingered in the air as Hester sat her doll down in the hallway for a talk.

"Can you smell that, little doll?" Hester sat on the floor next to the rag doll. "That's gonna be the best butter pound cake you ever tasted. It's Mama's special cake for when Grandmother Laura and Gran'daddy come over." Then Hester looked down at the little rag doll. "I know how to make mud cakes. And I can make them all by myself, too. They're easy. You just mix dirt flour and water, and bake them outside when the sun shines *real* hot." Hester giggled. "But they sure don't taste as good as Mama's cakes."

Hester scooped the doll up into her arms and off they went down the long, narrow hall. When Hester reached the door to her bedroom, she stopped and proudly announced, "This room is for you and me!" Then she frowned. "But we gotta share it with Annie, and sometimes she fusses. Like when she tells me to be extra quiet 'cause she's reading." Then Hester smiled. "But sometimes, before we go to sleep, Annie tells me stories.

Lots of stories, from books she reads." Hester whirled the little rag doll around and around. "Now you can hear them, too, little doll! *H-m-m* . . ." She paused for a moment. "I think it's time I find you a name . . . a special name, just like Grandmama Alfie said." Then she giggled. " 'Cause calling you 'little doll' sure doesn't sound so special." Hester sat down on her bed and rocked back and forth trying to think of a special name for her new doll. Until . . . Hester wrinkled her nose. "What's that *icky* smell?"

Suddenly, Mama's voice rang out from the kitchen, "Oh, my cake, my special cake. It's burnt!"

CHAPTER THREE

Spinning A Tale

AFTER A VERY solemn dinner during which Mama could only talk about her burnt cake, the girls quietly excused themselves to take their baths and dress for bed.

When Mama and Papa came to tuck them in, Hester was busy introducing her new doll to all of her other toys. She held the rag doll up to the toy shelf. "And that's Prima Donna. She's my favorite. But now," Hester said as she hugged the little rag doll, "you can be my favorite, too."

"All right, Hester. I'm sure they'll be *just* fine till the morning." Papa chuckled. "Hop in," he said as he pulled her bedcovers down. "It's time to say nighty-night."

After Papa tucked Hester in, he sat down on her bed. "Do you like the little doll, puddin'?" he asked.

Hester beamed. "Oh, yes, Papa!"

"Well, that's good to know." Papa pushed back the long brown curls from Hester's face. "Because Grandmama Alfie said that she sewed her together with bits and pieces of very special cloths."

"What kind of cloth?" Hester asked.

"Well, parts of your doll are made of things from my childhood, like her dress. It was cut from a shirt I wore when I was just a boy. And her apron used to be an old tablecloth that Grandmama Alfie used for special dinners. But the cloth for her body is the *most* special of all. It came from Grandmama Alfie's grandmother's dress. The one she wore when she was stolen from her village in Africa and brought here to America many, many years ago."

"Stolen?" said Annie, suddenly concerned as she sat up in bed and leaned over to listen better to Papa's story.

"Yes, stolen," Papa repeated.

Hester looked over to Mama, who stood nearby, then she hugged her doll even closer as Papa continued.

"You see, Grandmama Alfie's grandmother lived in a small village in West Africa. Her father made medicine and sang prayers that helped his people. They thought he had 'magic.' Grandmama Alfie's grandmother was your great-great-grandmother. Her name was Blessing. She was only twelve years old when she was stolen from her village and brought across a great ocean on an illegal slave ship. Once in America, she lived a very hard life. And for all her eighty-eight years on this earth, she longed for her father and her home in Africa."

"Blessing was stolen and brought across a great ocean," Papa said.

"That's such a sad story, Papa," Annie said, as she lay back down in her bed.

"Ah! But it's not." Papa continued. "You see, after she was taken from her father, he became so lonely that he called to the sun, the moon, and the stars and asked them to use their magic light to shine down on her always so that she wouldn't feel so lonely. To let her know that she was loved, no matter how far away she was."

Hester listened carefully, gently combing her fingers through the curly, woolen clusters on her doll's head as they talked more about their family's history.

"This is a story I want you girls to remember and tell *your* children one day," Papa said as he finished.

Mama leaned over and gave Hester a goodnight kiss. "Have you given your doll a name yet?"

"Yes, Mama. I'm going to call her *Minnie. Minnie Merriweather,*" Hester proudly announced.

Annie smirked. "And how did you think of *that* name?"

" 'Cause in Sunday school my teacher always says we should count our minnie blessings," Hester said thoughtfully.

"But she means the word M-A-N-Y," Annie protested. "Not a girl's name, silly!"

"Why, I think Minnie is a fine name, Hester," Papa reassured her.

Hester slowly nodded her head as she began to drift off to sleep. "Yes, Papa. I like it, too."

CHAPTER FOUR

Secrets

As Hester and Annie lay sleeping, a voice pierced the darkness.

"Why, may I ask, isn't she up here on the shelf with the rest of us, instead of in our dear Hester's bed?" snapped Prima Donna as she looked down at Minnie.

Although she was the prettiest doll, Prima Donna had the ugliest temper. She sat all the way up, on the very top shelf. That was so she wouldn't get her fancy pink dress dirty or crack her delicate porcelain face. Hester didn't play with Prima Donna much because she wasn't a "playing" doll. She was a "looking" doll. Prima Donna didn't mind. She wasn't very fond of being tousled about by really-for-real children anyway.

Prima Donna pouted. "Who does *she* think she is?"

"I think our dear Hester's father said she is, *umm* . . . ," Baby Doll said, hesitating for a moment. "Special."

"Special! What could possibly make *her* so special?" Prima Donna snarled. "Why, look at that ungainly creature. She is no more special than a common dust cloth."

"Why isn't she up here on the shelf with the rest of us?" snapped Prima Donna.

Minnie could hear the voices. *Toys can talk?* she thought. *That means I can talk too!* She tried to speak, but she couldn't think of what to say.

Suddenly, words rang out from a dark corner.

"Hey! Just 'cause she's a rag doll don't matter. Give her a chance, stop all that chatter."

Never taking her eyes off Minnie, Prima Donna answered, "Don't worry. That little rag-a-muffin will soon get her chance — a chance to join the rest of you 'used-to-be's.' "

At that very moment, Minnie put the words she needed with the thoughts she was having. "Now that wasn't a nice thing to say. Grandmama Alfie always said, 'Pretty is as pretty does.' "

The toys let out a loud gasp. Then a hush fell over the room. Since none of the toys had ever seen a handmade doll before, they weren't quite sure how she should behave. But they were *very* sure that no one ever spoke back to Prima Donna.

Baby Doll broke the silence. "You sure have a funny sounding voice."

They all had forgotten how strange a voice can sound when it is used for the very first time.

Minnie was just as surprised to hear it as they. Her voice was small, and light, and made little squeaky noises. In fact, using her new voice kind of tickled. And it made Minnie laugh! As she sat up to get a better look at the other toys, she lost her balance and rolled right off the bed. *Bumpity-bump-bump.* She landed in the most unflattering way. Her little, cotton-filled arms and legs were so twisted and turned that she looked more like an old rag than a doll.

"*Oops!*" Minnie cheerfully grinned as she lay there looking up at the other toys on the shelf.

Prima Donna smirked. "Hmm. Now that was very *special.*"

Minnie tried to stand, but her legs kept giving way. Like her voice, they were wobbly since she had never used them before either.

"Do, dah, dah-do!" She laughed as she practiced using her new voice. "Now I can take all of the stuff in here," Minnie pointed to her cotton-filled head, "and let you hear it!" Then Minnie's eyes widened. "I wonder though. Will I use up all the thoughts in my head if I let you hear them, too?"

"Preposterous," growled Grumpy Old Bear, who wasn't the least bit amused that he had been disturbed from his sleep. "What a silly thing to say. Thoughts are thoughts and words are words."

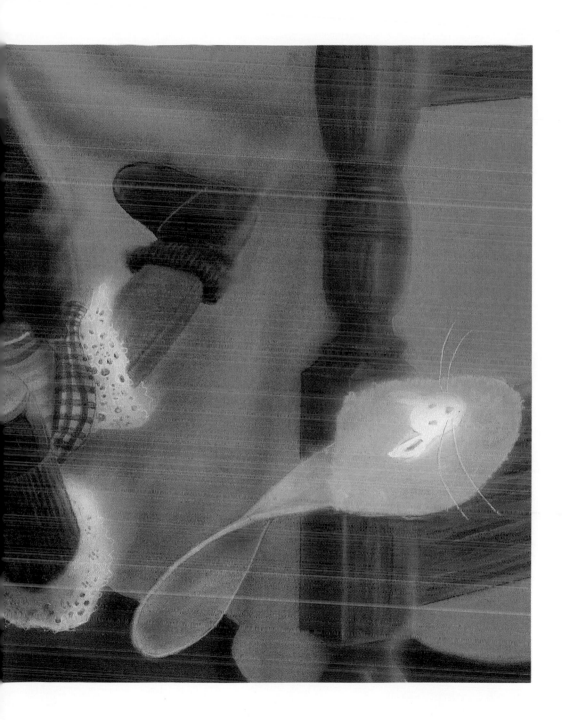

The voice from the corner spoke again. This time it added a warning: "Best wait to talk and run about, till all the really-for-real folks are out. If you're hankerin' to play late at night, long past the time when they've turned off the lights, best wait till they're for sure asleep. 'Cause when they're 'wake, *shhh!* Not even a peep."

Minnie looked for the rhyming voice in the corner. "Well, how do we know for sure that the really-for-real folks can't hear us?"

"We just know, that's all," Grumpy Old Bear said impatiently.

"They can only hear us when we make a big fuss, like you've just done!" snapped Prima Donna.

"Why, yes," Baby Doll said. "And you must be ever so careful that you don't let them catch you."

Minnie shuddered. "Oh my. What would happen if they did?"

"We don't know," said Waddle Waddle, the wooden pull-toy duck, in a frightened voice. "We've never known any toy who has been seen moving about by really-for-real folks."

"Aw, Minnie. They *think* they know lots more than you," said the voice from the corner once again. "Just remember what I said to do."

Minnie brushed back the yarn that dangled over her eye as she tried to get a better look at who was talking.

"Who are you?" Minnie asked the voice. "Can you come out and play?"

Minnie looked for the rhyming voice in the corner.

Prima Donna spoke at once. "Of course he can't come out and play. He's just one of Annie's forgotten toys." Looking toward the dark corner, she added, "You used to be her favorite. But you're a nobody now."

"Yeah?" the voice shot back. "Well, truth is it suits me to stay a 'used-to-be' any ol' day. At least I have nice words to say. You're just made from fancy dressin', always tryin' to be impressin'."

A hush swept over the room.

"*Ah-hum.*" Waddle Waddle cleared his throat and glanced at Prima Donna.

"Careful," Prima Donna warned. "I'm the one who's speaking now."

"Uh! Of course, Miss Prima," Waddle Waddle said nervously. "Of course."

"As for you, little Miss Rag-a-muffin," Prima Donna said, turning back to Minnie. "Don't think you can make *us* forgotten toys. You think you're 'special' now, but you better remember your place. You're just another toy." Then Prima Donna gave Minnie the meanest glare. "Otherwise, you may find yourself a NEVER-FOUND!"

Minnie sat on the floor with a thud. " 'Never-found'? That sure sounds awful bad."

"Yes. It's the most horrible fate a toy can have," Baby Doll said in a fearful voice. "That's what happened to our dearly loved Gusandra Goose."

Grumpy Old Bear shook his head and frowned. "Poor Gusandra Goose."

There was a long, sad pause. Why, the looks on the toys' faces were so sad they made Minnie cry.

"For goodness sake." Prima Donna looked down at Minnie. "Why on earth are you crying? You didn't even know the ol' goose!"

"Don't cry, Minnie." Waddle Waddle took a deep breath. And with all the courage he could muster up, he said, "Come on. I'll play with you."

"I've already warned you!" announced Prima Donna.

Before Waddle Waddle knew what was happening, Prima Donna gave him a swift shove. Right off the shelf.

He crashed to the floor with the loudest clatter. BOOM! BAM! THUD! He bounced and bumped and rolled straight across the floor, and the only thing that stopped him was the bedroom door.

Hester and Annie stirred in their beds but did not wake.

"Oh, dear." Grumpy Old Bear raised his paws to his cheeks. "That will surely wake the really-for-real folks. I just know it."

Suddenly, they all heard footsteps, really-for-real folks' footsteps. The sounds came closer. The knob on the bedroom door began to turn, and the door slowly opened. Light from the hallway streaked across Waddle Waddle on the floor.

"Now I wonder what happened here," Mama said as she entered the room and looked at the wooden duck lying in front of the door.

She picked up Waddle Waddle and placed him back on the top shelf, never stopping to turn on the light. As Mama turned

to leave, she stepped right on Minnie. But this didn't hurt Minnie a bit. Toys don't feel pain like really-for-real folks.

"Oh! And what's this?" Mama reached down in the darkness and lifted the little rag doll from the floor. "For goodness sake. What are *you* doing down here, Minnie?"

Mama placed the doll back into Hester's bed. "Now, go to sleep. No more playing for you tonight. I've got a big day tomorrow." She pulled the cover up over Hester's shoulders. "Don't know what I'm going to do about the cake." She sighed as she looked at Minnie once more. "There I go again, worrying about that cake." Mama paused and shook her head. "Oh dear, just listen to me. I sound just like Hester, talking to this doll like she's real."

Then she left, closing the door behind her.

All the toys stayed quiet. That had been a close call.

Minnie felt herself grow sleepy. What a big day it had been. Her first train ride, new friends, and now a secret world to explore. Pleasant thoughts and plans filled her soft, cotton-filled head as Minnie drifted peacefully off to sleep.

CHAPTER FIVE

Baker's Monday

"**W**AKE UP! Wake up!" Hester tugged on Annie's arm. "Mama said to get dressed so she can drop you off at Miss Earlene's house to get your hair done."

"Oh, stop pulling my arm, Hester," moaned Annie, still half-asleep.

"Mama! Mama!" Hester yelled. "Annie won't get up."

"Yes I will," Annie yelled back as she dragged herself from the bed. "*Tattletale,*" she whispered to Hester.

Hester, who was already dressed, pretended not to hear Annie. She just kept humming and giggling and talking to Minnie while she fluffed her smock.

"Now, Minnie, remember, we have to be on our best behavior when Mrs. Morgan comes. Okay, my little Minnie?" Hester gave the doll a big hug. "If you're extra good, I'll give you a special surprise." Hester held out her pinkie finger. "Pinkie promise."

Annie tried her best to ignore Hester. But she couldn't.

"Hester, that's just a doll. You're treating her like she's *real*.

She's not any more *special* than the other toys on your shelf,"
Annie blurted out.

"She is *so* special. 'Cause Papa said so. Remember the
story?" Hester tried not to show Annie she had hurt her
feelings.

"Come on, Annie," Mama called from the front room.

At that moment, someone knocked at the front door. When
Mama answered it, there stood Mrs. Morgan. She was a plump
woman with a smile that could light up the gloomiest day.

"Good morning, Willimena," Mrs. Morgan said in a strong
voice.

"Why, good morning to you, Mrs. Morgan. Heard you're doing much better."

"Fair to middlin'," Mrs. Morgan said. "But that's all right. Lord willin', with a lot of liniment and a little prayer, I'll be up to snuff in no time." Mrs. Morgan chuckled. "Besides, I don't have time to tarry. Got too much to do."

They both laughed.

"Mrs. Morgan, would you make sure that Hester gets her full nap today? My mother and father are coming for dinner tonight and I want her to be at her best," Mama said.

"Don't worry, Willimena, I know that child's got more energy than a jackrabbit. But I'll make sure she sleeps well today," Mrs. Morgan assured Mama.

"Oh! And if Mr. Merriweather gets home early, feel free to go. I know you've got things to do as well," Mama said.

Mama hugged and kissed Hester. Then she and Annie quickly went down the stairs.

Mrs. Morgan turned to Hester, who was holding Minnie.

"Good morning to you, little Miss Hester," Mrs. Morgan said. "And what do we have here?" She looked down at the rag doll Hester held.

"She's my new best friend. Her name is Minnie. Minnie Merriweather," Hester said with pride.

"Is that so?" Mrs. Morgan said. "And where did Minnie come from?"

"Good morning to you, little Miss Hester," Mrs. Morgan said.

"My Grandmama Alfie made her. She's special." Hester beamed as she spoke.

"Well, now. Is that so?" Mrs. Morgan smiled as she studied the doll closer. "And what do you and Minnie want to do today?"

"Can we do anything we want, Mrs. Morgan?" Hester asked.

Mrs. Morgan paused for a moment. "As long as it don't take a heap of energy. You know Mrs. Morgan ain't as young as she used to be." Then she put her arm around Hester. "Now, what is it you want to do, child?"

"Bake a cake. A real cake. 'Cause Mama's didn't turn out so good yesterday."

"Oh, now that seems like a fine idea," Mrs. Morgan said. "That would make your Mama real happy. Let's see what we need first, then we'll head on down to Mr. Solomon's store to get all the makings." Mrs. Morgan sat down to make a list.

After Mrs. Morgan, Hester, and Minnie had finished shopping and returned to the apartment, Mrs. Morgan glanced at the clock on the wall.

"Oh, my goodness!" she said as she finished laying the groceries out on the kitchen counter. "Where did time fly? My program comes on in two minutes. Go turn on the radio in the front room, sugar," she said to Hester. "I'll be right in as soon as I light the oven. When my soap opera goes off, we'll mix and bake the cake."

Hester quickly went into the front room and over to the RCA Victor cabinet radio. She turned the left knob until it clicked, then grabbed a pillow and took a seat on the floor with Minnie. In an instant, Mrs. Morgan came in and sat in her favorite stuffed armchair. They all listened quietly as the voice spoke from the radio:

"For a wash that's white without bleaching," the radio announcer began, "use Snowflake, with its lively active hustle bubble suds." The dramatic organ music swelled. "Snowflake and the NBC Blue Network are pleased to bring you 'The Irene Rich Dramas.'" And the music continued.

CHAPTER SIX

A Sweet Surprise

HESTER noticed that Mrs. Morgan wasn't talking
back to the voices on the radio anymore. She was
snoring. Hester knew she shouldn't wake her. She
remembered what Mama had said about letting Mrs. Morgan
get her rest. But Hester also knew that if Mama and Annie
came home before Mrs. Morgan woke up, she wouldn't get her
chance to bake the cake.

"Minnie," Hester said. "I wish we could surprise Mrs.
Morgan and Mama and make that cake. Just you and me, don't
you?" Then Hester made Minnie's head nod "yes."

Hester clutched Minnie's hand and walked into the
kitchen. She looked around. Everything looked so strange.
There were so many pots and pans and things. "I wonder what
we do first?" Hester paused for a moment. "*Hmmm.* Mama
always looks at her cookbook." Hester took Minnie over to the
kitchen table and sat down. She quickly opened the oversized
book to the page Mama had left marked with a spoon.

Hester carefully placed her finger under each word. "Cream butter and sugar T-O-G-E-T-H-E-R. Add two eggs and one cup of S-I-F-T-E-D flour." Hester sat straight up in the seat, took a deep breath, and kept reading. "Mix T-O-G-E- . . . Put your oven's T-E-M- . . ." Hester frowned. Although Hester was the best reader in her class, she couldn't read enough of the words in Mama's recipe book to make the butter pound cake. "Maybe we better wait for Mrs. Morgan after all, Minnie." Hester sighed.

As they sat there listening to the quiet *ticktock* of the kitchen clock, Hester began to yawn.

Minnie stared straight ahead. *I bet I can help,* she thought. *Grandmama Alfie made cakes. But I don't remember her looking at any books to make them. Why do you need a book to make a cake?*

Sitting in the warm kitchen, Hester struggled to keep her eyes opened. Finally, she put her arms on the tabletop and laid her head down. "Maybe we'll just sit here till I can think of what to do." She yawned again. "But for sure, making a real cake is way different than making mud cakes." Hester closed her eyes and fell fast asleep.

Minnie waited until she knew for sure that Hester was

sound asleep before she slipped off her lap. Then, she tiptoed over to the counter where Mrs. Morgan had laid out the groceries. She climbed up the handles of the drawers to take a better look around.

"*Hmmm.* Now, let's see," Minnie said as she sat up on the counter and rested her back against the flour sack. She wasn't quite certain just where to begin. She scratched her cotton-filled head. "Grandmama Alfie always sang a song when she baked. Maybe that's what I need to do." Minnie sprang to her feet. "I'll sing a song!" But then she remembered. "I don't know any."

In Hester's bedroom, all of the toys were having a wonderful tea party. None of them knew a thing about what Minnie was up to. Prima Donna was busy holding court as she sat at the head of the tiny doll table.

Since there were only two chairs, Prima Donna had all the toys take turns sitting at the table. As she invited them to sit, one at a time, she pretended to offer them tea and cakes.

Grumpy Old Bear, who was always hungry, was getting rather impatient waiting for his turn. "This is a silly idea," he grumbled. "Why, there isn't even any tea in those cups or cakes on those plates."

In Hester's bedroom, all of the toys were having a wonderful tea party.

"He's right," Baby Doll said. "This isn't a *real* tea party without tea and cakes."

"Well," said Waddle Waddle. "Let's go into the kitchen and get all the things we need so we *can* have a *real* tea party!"

"Great idea!" said Grumpy Old Bear.

"Yes," agreed Baby Doll.

All the toys began talking at once.

"Silence!" Prima Donna had listened to just about enough of their chattering. "This is supposed to be *my* tea party."

While Prima Donna was calling the tea party back to order, no one noticed that one of the "forgotten" toys had wriggled out of Annie's toy chest.

"All this talk of delicious food, sure puts me in a hungry mood," the forgotten toy mumbled as he slipped from the room and headed for the kitchen.

Minnie was busy at work in the kitchen.

"This sack of flour sure is hard to open," she said to herself as she yanked and yanked on the thin cord that dangled from its stitched top.

"If only I could . . . ," Minnie said as she gave it one . . . last . . . tug.

As Minnie pulled the cord with all her might, she began to

lose her balance. *"Uh! Oh!"* she cried out, teetering back and forth over the edge of the counter. Suddenly, Minnie lost her balance completely. *"Weee!"* She squealed with delight as she held tight to the cord and swung from side to side, twisting and turning, laughing all the while. Minnie was so dizzy twirling, so busy laughing, she hadn't noticed the gunnysack moving inch-by-inch-by-inch . . . until . . . it inched right off the counter!

Kaboom! *SPLAT!*

Thick, billowy white clouds filled the room. As it settled to the floor, the flour covered Minnie like a blanket of freshly fallen snow, burying her completely. Poking her head through the mountain of flour, she began to laugh. "Well, that's surely one way to open a sack of flour."

From the doorway she heard a chuckle.

"Who's there?" Minnie asked as she wiped the flour dust from her eyes.

"It's me, Scruffy," the voice said.

"How do you do? Come closer so I can see you better," Minnie said in a soft, floury voice.

"But I don't look brand-spankin' new, like Hester's toys do. See, I'm just Annie's old stuffed rabbit and sometimes I like talkin' in rhymes, just outta habit."

Scruffy's golden brown fur was well worn. His ears pointed in different directions. There was a faded brass windup key that stuck out from his right side. Before its spring broke, it played Annie's favorite nursery song, "Twinkle Twinkle Little Star." But now it was just a sad reminder of why he had become a used-to-be.

Minnie looked him over. "Why, you look just dandy to me." Scruffy blushed and quickly hopped over to Minnie. "We best get goin', lickety-split. But first we should spruce you up a bit. 'Cause when Hester wakes she'll have a fit. And besides, all Hester's toys are headin' this way, wantin' to get fixin's for a party today."

"But, Scruffy," Minnie sighed. "I've just got to figure out how to make this cake for our dear Hester and her mother. Can you help me?"

"Me? Help? Sure! Scruffy's my name. But fixin' problems is my game."

Though Scruffy really wasn't sure just what he could do, it certainly felt good to be useful again.

Cling. Clang. Cling-idy-clang.

"What on earth could that be?" Grumpy Old Bear grumbled.

"Well let's not *dillydally*," Waddle Waddle urged. "Whatever it is, it's not coming from the really-for-real folks. That's for sure." Somehow they always seemed to know things like that.

Still, the toys cautiously scurried down the hallway. As they approached the kitchen door, the noise grew louder.

"It's coming from inside the kitchen," Baby Doll said.

Prima Donna nudged Waddle Waddle. "Well, since you told us not to *dillydally,* you take a look."

"I, *uh*, I," Waddle Waddle stammered.

"*Humph.* Really. Afraid, just as I thought," Prima Donna said.

Prima Donna slowly pushed open the door, just as Scruffy and Minnie were pouring a thick, rich batter into the carefully lined wax papered pan.

"Well, isn't this a tender moment," Prima Donna said scornfully as she motioned the other toys behind her to take a look.

"What are they doing?" Grumpy Old Bear said as he stepped forward.

"I think we've just made our first really-for-real cake!" Minnie announced triumphantly.

"Yeah! See!" Scruffy picked up Mama's cookbook. "Just like the one in this book. Come on over and take a look!"

The toys gathered around the book and looked at the picture of the cake. Then without another word, Scruffy hopped over to the stove. He bounced and bounced and bounced . . . until . . . he finally was able to grab the oven door, pulling it open as he landed on the kitchen floor.

Minnie quickly turned the mixing bowl upside down and dragged it in front of the warm oven. Then she picked up the pan filled with the cake batter and climbed on top of the bowl in order to place the pan inside.

"Whoa!" Minnie tried not to spill the batter as she steadied her wobbly legs on the slippery ceramic bowl.

"Careful," Scruffy warned. "Keep it real straight and steady. 'Cause after it's in, we can't check till it's ready."

Grumpy Old Bear's stomach growled. "I'd be more than happy to sample a piece when it's done," he said.

After Minnie closed the oven door, her excitement quickly turned to dismay as she looked around the kitchen. "Oh my. Look at this mess."

"Well," Prima Donna said. "I told you toys that's all she's good for, making one mess after another."

"Careful," Scruffy warned. "Keep it real straight and steady."

Prima Donna's shrill laugh made the other toys follow in chorus.

"Aw, look, she ain't done nothin' to you." Scruffy put his worn-out paw on Minnie's shoulder. "The only thing she's wantin' to do, is play and be good friends with you. And look at how you all laugh and tease. When all she's tryin' to do is please."

All the toys began to mumble in agreement.

Baby Doll spoke up from behind Prima Donna. "Scruffy's right, she's nice. And she seems like she's fun to play with, too."

Before Waddle Waddle spoke he made certain he was nowhere near Prima Donna. "Yes. Let's all help," he said.

"*Humph.* Go ahead," Prima Donna sneered. "As for me? I *absolutely* cannot get my dress soiled. After all, it's not like that cotton mill dress little Miss Rag-a-muffin's wearing."

The other toys turned as one toward Prima Donna. The looks on their faces didn't need words.

But Baby Doll spoke up anyway. "I don't think that was a very nice thing to say."

"Rude and selfish is what it was," added Grumpy Old Bear.

Waddle Waddle nodded and said, "That's right." Then he quickly ducked behind Grumpy Old Bear.

Prima Donna was quite surprised by their reaction. "What . . . I . . . er . . ." She hesitated for a moment. "What I *meant* was that our dear Hester would be terribly upset if my dress got soiled. It *is* made from the finest silk, you know."

"And what a pretty dress it is, Miss Prima," Minnie said.

Prima Donna paused again, then muttered a slightly embarrassed *"Humph."*

Minnie turned her attention back to the mess, trying to figure out what to do next.

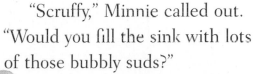

"Scruffy," Minnie called out. "Would you fill the sink with lots of those bubbly suds?"

Scruffy puffed his chest out. Proud to be chosen first, he happily hopped onto the counter and poured the entire box of soap flakes under the running tap water.

Soon, rainbow-colored soap bubbles filled the air. The toys delighted in chasing after them. All the toys except Prima Donna, of course.

Pop! Pop! Pop! went the glass-like bubbles, bursting almost as fast as they escaped from under the faucet. This amused the toys so; they began to laugh loudly, completely forgetting about Hester, who was napping at the kitchen table. Until . . .

"*Ummm.*" Hester began to gently stir.

The toys stood still until they were *very* certain Hester was still asleep.

"I think we better hurry and help Minnie before our dear Hester wakes," Baby Doll said in a soft voice.

All of the toys agreed and went back to the job of tidying up the kitchen.

Minnie took one of the dish towels from the hook and began to wipe the counter.

"I'll sweep up the flour," Baby Doll said as she grabbed the small dust brush.

Not to be outdone, Waddle Waddle quacked, "And I'll pick up all these eggshells." Rolling crisscross across the floor, he used his beak like a dustpan, scooping up all the chunks and small bits of shell.

Prima Donna noticed Grumpy Old Bear without a chore. "And what will you do, old bear?" she chided.

"Why, I'm going to . . . to . . ." But as Grumpy Old Bear looked around, he couldn't see anything else that needed to be done.

"You could hold the trash can open," Prima Donna said with amusement. "That certainly seems like a job worthy of *your* efforts."

In fact, it did seem like the only job left to do.

So Grumpy Old Bear decided to stand grandly with his foot pressed down on the trash can's pedal. His arms gallantly

folded across his chest, he tried to make his job seem far more important than it really was.

The toys swept and scrubbed and polished, until everything was as it was before.

"*Mmmm.*" Hester began to rouse from her nap.

"*Our dear Hester's waking!*" Baby Doll whispered. "*We'd better go back to our toy shelf!*"

Suddenly, the sound of footsteps was heard on the stairs. Really-for-real folks' footsteps!

"Oh, dear! Oh, dear!" Grumpy Old Bear groaned nervously. "Now the really-for-real folks will catch us for sure. I just know it."

"Let's not *dillydally!*" Waddle Waddle said as he rolled down the long hallway.

"I don't think we're going to make it," Baby Doll cried.

Halfway down the hall, Grumpy Old Bear stopped to catch his breath. "And to think, I never got a chance to eat any of that yummy cake," he puffed.

Suddenly, the toys heard the jingling of keys on the other side of the door. Grumpy Old Bear held his breath and didn't move.

"Take your time, Annie," Mama said, as they stood outside their front door. Mama was patiently holding an armful of packages while Annie fumbled with Mama's keys.

"Why do parents always have to have so many different keys on the same ring?" Annie complained, still trying to find the right one.

"Here," Mama finally said as she put the packages down. "Let me see them."

In all of the excitement, no one noticed Scruffy's tail caught in the kitchen door. Not even Minnie. By the time Minnie did hear Scruffy's faint calls for help, she was already sitting nicely in Hester's lap.

"*Scruffy!*" Minnie softly called back.

Prima Donna was the last to leave. Hearing Minnie's call she turned around, catching sight of Scruffy trying to wriggle free.

"Scruffy! What are you up to?" Prima Donna scolded. "Get back to that old chest of yours this instant!"

"Can't," Scruffy grunted, still trying to loosen his tail. "Awful bad luck, I'm downright stuck."

Before Prima Donna could do or say another thing, the key turned and the door unlocked. She dashed down the hallway, barely ahead of Mama and Annie as they entered.

"*Mmmm*. Smells good," Annie said.

"You were right. It was coming from our apartment, Annie."

Mama and Annie headed for the kitchen through the front room.

Mrs. Morgan was just waking.

"How'd everything go, Willimena?" Mrs. Morgan asked, still half-asleep.

"Just fine, Mrs. Morgan. And what's that I smell?"

Mrs. Morgan took a deep sniff. "Oh my! It smells like the cake baking!"

Everyone rushed into the kitchen.

"Why Mrs. Morgan," Mama said as she went over to the oven and peeked inside. "A butter pound cake! What a thoughtful thing to do."

Before Mrs. Morgan had a chance to speak Mama turned and gave her a great big hug.

Mrs. Morgan was a bit confused. She didn't remember mixing the batter, let alone putting the cake into the oven. But she couldn't let Mama know that, so she just smiled and said, "Well, truth be told it was Hester's idea, Willimena."

Mama looked over at Hester, who was just waking from her nap. Mama pulled up a chair and sat down next to her.

"Darling." Mama gently coaxed Hester awake. "Was it your idea to make the cake?"

Hester sat up and rubbed the sleep from her eyes. "*Uh-huh,*" said Hester, nodding. Then she took in a deep breath as sweet smells of baked butter and vanilla filled her nose.

"Well, it certainly seems that you understand a lot more than I give you credit for." Mama hugged Hester.

Annie just shook her head. "It's about time she thought about something other than that silly doll."

Neither Mrs. Morgan nor Hester really knew what had happened, so they kept a puzzled silence.

And as for Minnie? Well, she was trying very hard not to

"Now, what do we have here?" Mrs. Morgan asked.

giggle, but she sure was busting at the seams with pride.

"Now, what do we have here?" Mrs. Morgan asked as she noticed something stuck in the door.

"It's Scruffy!" Annie rushed over to get him. "I'd forgotten all about you." Then Annie's eyes darted over to Hester. "Hey, what is he doing out of my toy chest anyway?"

"Annie," Mama quickly interrupted. "Isn't it about time you let Hester enjoy some of your old toys? I'm sure they must be very lonely locked up in that chest all of the time. Don't you think?"

Annie paused. Then she realized Mama was probably right. Hester would enjoy them better. Besides, for her, they were just toys that used-to-be fun.

"Oh, all right," Annie said as she handed the old, stuffed toy rabbit to Hester. "You better take good care of him and not lose him like you did Gusandra Goose! Scruffy was my favorite, you know."

"Gee! Thanks, Annie!" Hester said. "And you're my favorite sister, too, you know."

"I'm your *only* sister, silly," Annie said with a grin.

They both laughed.

CHAPTER SEVEN

Magic

Later that night, long after Grandmother Laura and Gran'daddy, full of delicious cake, were gone and the Merriweather family was fast asleep, two shadowy figures sat on the windowsill of Hester and Annie's bedroom, whispering in the dark.

"Minnie, we sure had an excitin' day, with a passel of thrills and plenty of play!"

"Sure did, Scruffy."

"Why, I'm as happy as a fly on a pie. It's so good to be out that ol' chest, even if I don't look my very best." Scruffy stared out into the night. "Guess you learned a bunch 'bout that special kind of magic, huh?"

"Magic?" Minnie repeated.

"Yeah." Scruffy seemed a bit distracted as he began counting the stars that twinkled in the light of the moon.

"Do you mean that tingly stuff I feel right here . . . inside?" Minnie patted her stuffed chest.

"Yep. That's what I'm talkin' 'bout. It's made from a special brew — good thoughts mixed with lots of warm feelings, too."

"But . . . how can I keep them?"

"Same way we did today," Scruffy said. "That cake you made showed you care 'bout others, like the happiness you brought to your dear Hester's mother."

"She's your dear Hester now, too, you know," Minnie promptly corrected him.

Right then, Scruffy's nose began to twitch and his ears started waving back and forth very fast. They did that when he was especially pleased. Minnie couldn't help but giggle as Scruffy struggled to hold his ears still, without much success.

Then Minnie's amusement faded. After a moment she asked, "But what about Prima Donna? She doesn't seem to feel that *special* way."

"Well, you see, it's just the way she's made to be." Scruffy put his paw around Minnie's shoulder. "Don't pay Prima Donna no never mind. She's gotta be taught to be thoughtful and kind. The really-for-real folks call it 'love.' And that's what this house is packed full of."

"Love." Minnie smiled. "I like that word."

"Just remember," Scruffy said, "it's gotta be shared . . . 'cause the magic only works when folks know you care."

"Sure thing, Scruffy. But I wonder . . . if I share my love with everyone all the time, will I use it all up?" Minnie seemed quite concerned.

Giggles sounded faintly from the toy shelf.

Right then, Scruffy's ears started waving back and forth very fast.

"Preposterous," grumbled Grumpy Old Bear.

"Nah," Scruffy said, pretending not to hear the other toys. "That's what makes it special b'yond compare. As long as you give it, it will always be there."

All the toys on the shelf listened carefully as Scruffy and Minnie continued their late-night whispers. Even Prima Donna seemed to pay attention, but who knows what she *really* understood.

After their talk was over, Minnie looked out at the starry night sky. Before she fell asleep she thought how special it was to have two families to love, the toys and the really-for-real folks, especially Hester. And though Minnie didn't know it yet, a new and exciting adventure was waiting for her, just ahead, in the wonderful world of make-believe.

Chocolate-Covered
Memories

Chocolate-Covered Memories

A SNAPSHOT

OF CHICAGO'S

AFRICAN-AMERICAN HISTORY

The Adventures of Minnie takes place in Chicago in 1933. Let's step back in time to Hester and Annie's world and learn more about it through historical accounts and oral retellings by Black women who were young girls growing up in Chicago's Bronzeville community in the 1930s.

The Arthur family arriving in Chicago on August 30, 1920, from Paris, Texas.

Robert Abbott, a lawyer who migrated from Savannah, Georgia, and established his newspaper, the "Chicago Defender," in 1905.

A large number of Chicago's African-American population arrived there by way of trains and buses departing daily from many Southern cities and rural communities. These people called Chicago "The Promised Land." This huge movement, known as the Great Migration, began at the start of the twentieth century. By the 1920s almost a million people had moved North, and the movement was still going strong at the time this story takes place, the 1930s. Southern Blacks came in search of jobs and better living conditions for their families. Many came because of stories they read in the *Chicago Defender*, which was a national weekly newspaper published for a Black audience. This newspaper tried to educate its readers about matters such as equality and freedom of choice, something many Southern Blacks were not allowed to experience.

Newspaper carrier, 1933. The subscription rate for one month was 35¢.

70

"Kitchenette" family in Chicago, 1938.

The densely populated group of neighborhoods where most Black Chicagoans lived was known as the Black Belt, but by the time the Merriweathers lived there, African Americans were calling it by a special name: Bronzeville. This name gave the community a sense of dignity and pride.

The neighborhoods of Bronzeville were made up of many kinds of housing. Some were "kitchenette" buildings with cramped one- and two-room apartments. Families who lived there often had to share a bathroom. Other kinds of apartment buildings were called "courtways." These were large U-shaped buildings, many with gated entranceways and grassy garden areas in the center. Hester and her family were happy to live in one of these buildings. Some families even lived in single-family homes that majestically lined large boulevards like Michigan Avenue and South Parkway.

Not all of Chicago's African Americans settled there during the Great Migration. Many Black families had been there for generations and were firmly established in the community. Lawyers, doctors, and businesspeople were all part of Bronzeville.

South Parkway, 1929 (later renamed Martin Luther King Drive). Many affluent African Americans lived and owned homes on streets like this.

Professionals like Dr. Daniel Hale Williams, the first doctor to successfully perform open-heart surgery, had the respect of all Chicagoans, both Black and White.

7% Yearly on the Overton Building First Mortgage Gold Bonds

Principal and interest payable in Chicago at the Douglass National Bank in United States gold coin of the present standard of weight and fineness.

THE OVERTON BUILDING

W E have erected a monument; a building inside and outside that will stand as a memorial to Negro enterprise and thrift. The building illustrated is the architect's drawing.

Location

This building is located on State Street, the principal thoroughfare in the City of Chicago; convenient to all parts of the city, and within easy access to the best and fastest transportation facilities. Located at 36th street, in the very heart of Colored activities of Chicago, and only twelve minutes to Chicago's great business center or "Loop"—the greatest retail district in the world.

The building occupies the block bounded on the West by State Street, on the North by

Overton Court, on the South by Thirty-Sixth Place, with an alley on the East. This property is owned by the Overton-Hygienic Mfg. Company, the largest manufacturing enterprise in the United States, owned and operated exclusively by Colored People; sole originators and producers of the famous line of HIGH-BROWN TOILET PREPARATIONS. References: R. G. Dun & Co., The Bradstreet Co., or any bank or banker.

Proprietary

The building and grounds are owned by the Overton Building Corporation.

Building

This is the finest building ever erected and owned by Colored people — reinforced concrete

Anthony Overton (1865–1946). Born into slavery in Monroe, Louisiana, Overton was educated at Washburn College and received a law degree from the University of Kansas. He established the Overton Hygienic Company (an international cosmetic company), a magazine called "Half-Century," the "Chicago Bee" newspaper, the Victory Life Insurance Company, and the Douglass National Bank.

In 1898, Overton started his first company with $1,960. By 1927 Dun & Bradstreet reported its worth at $1 million, with over 250 products being made, including those for other people's companies.

An advertisement for Overton's products, 1925. One of the company's most famous products was High-Brown facial powder, sought the world over. No other company made a face powder specifically for women of color.

In Bronzeville it wasn't unusual for Black upper- and middle-class families to live in the same building or next door to families who were barely making ends meet. Chicago's African-American community was packed largely into one area because of the city's Restrictive Agreement, a covenant that prohibited

Blacks from moving into White neighborhoods. The invisible boundaries of the
covenant stretched south from 26th
Street to 63rd Street, and east from
Cottage Grove Avenue to State Street.

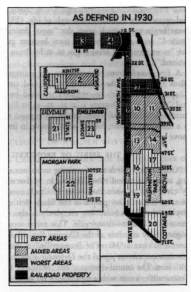

*Signs like this let
potential tenants
know a building
was going to
change occupancy
from White to
Black tenants,
1938. This is just
one example of
how the
Restrictive
Agreement was
carried out*

*In 1930, St. Clair Drake and Horace
Cayton, authors of "Black
Metropolis," identified and defined
conditions in areas within the Black
Belt and other communities where
African Americans resided.*

Though home and community had a
different meaning to each family, children from various backgrounds
often played together, went to the same school, and enjoyed the same
social centers. Despite all their differences, neighbors still looked
after neighbors and always paid special attention to the children.

"I never thought about safety when I was a young girl. The worst thing I
feared was one of the neighbors telling my mother that they saw me some-
where I wasn't supposed to be."
— JUNE (JOHNSON) FINCH

*Children playing ring-
around-the-rosy, Chicago,
1938.*

Unlike the men in this advertisement, Pullman porters had very little to smile about before the Brotherhood of Sleeping Car Porters was formed on August 25, 1925. Unfair wages and working conditions prompted a small group of Black Pullman porters to ask A. Philip Randolph, editor of "The Messenger," a Black labor magazine, to help organize their group and win a legitimate place in the Pullman Union. On August 25, 1937, twelve years after Randolph helped to organize the Brotherhood, it became the first Black union to sign a labor contract with a major corporation.

At the time the Merriweathers lived in Bronzeville, Chicago, that city, as well as the rest of the country, found itself in the grip of the Great Depression. Money was scarce and many of the nation's banks had closed their doors. Those Americans who did have jobs were desperate to keep them. In Bronzeville, morticians and Pullman porters, like Hester's father, often had better paying jobs than many dentists, doctors, or lawyers. It wasn't unusual for a Black man with a college degree to sort and deliver mail or wait on White passengers on the trains. Often Pullman porters earned enough in tips and wages to keep their families in a very comfortable style. If money could be earned, the economic hardship could be kept away.

"We owned our home at 6343 Champlain. My mother was a schoolteacher. My father was a dining-car porter on the Milwaukee line. I'd love when he'd make his long runs to Seattle. He'd always bring back big, king-sized oysters. They were my favorite. I never thought much about the Depression except what we could see in the newspaper. It wasn't something that was part of our lives."

—JUNE (JOHNSON) FINCH

Pullman porters in the early 1930s at Chicago's Central Station, 12th Street.

The Depression did affect most people. It took away their jobs and their dignity. Though pocketbooks and wallets shrank, hearts often seemed to grow bigger. People never knew if they might be the next to lose their job, so they usually tried to show kindness to those who were in need.

"My mother was a chief cook and my father was a chef in the big downtown hotels. The Depression was not something we knew except from the stories my mother would tell us. I remember one day

Publisher Robert Abbott and staff, standing in front of the "Defender" building to give away food to needy families, Thanksgiving week 1931.

she told us about seeing entire families walking around, looking for food in the garbage bin in back of the hotel where she worked. From that day on, my mother would make certain that she instructed the kitchen helpers to take the leftover food off the plates and put it on a large tray instead of in the garbage. Then my mother would set the trays outside so that these people would at least be able to keep part of their dignity. And though it was food off someone else's plate, it would not be mixed with dirt and debris." — MYRTLE (BENSON) MALLORY

"The only thing we knew [about the Depression] was that some of our relatives would come by with their relief [welfare] boxes filled with dry grains and goods and our Mother would give them cash money for it. She did that so they could go and buy fresh meats and vegetables for their own family."

— GWENDOLYN KING

Bread lines like this were seen in every city and crossed racial lines during the Depression.

For most families in 1933, money was in short supply. One popular pastime for family home entertainment was listening to the radio. In the afternoons and evenings, children and adults would cozy up and listen to the adventures of such favorite characters as Little Orphan Annie, the Lone Ranger, or Mandrake the Magician.

Soap operas like *One Man's Family* and *The Goldbergs* took listeners away from their own problems and into someone else's life. The most popular radio show of the time, *Amos 'n' Andy*, was actually set in Bronzeville. Though originally the actors in these shows were White, their humor succeeded in entertaining audiences of all races.

Liberty Life Insurance, a Black-owned company, housed a radio studio (above). Programs were aired Monday through Friday at 10 P.M. on their station, WWAE (inset photo).

Sound effects made radio shows even more exciting. Listeners could never have imagined how many people it took to create realistic background sounds.

Musical variety shows were also popular. The *Ziegfeld Follies of the Air* and *The Eddie Cantor Show* brought stage and screen stars into people's homes without the costly price of a ticket. NBC aired a live program from Chicago's most popular Black nightclub, featuring Black stars such as Butterbeans and Susie, The Four Stairsteps, Lena Horne, and Ethel Waters.

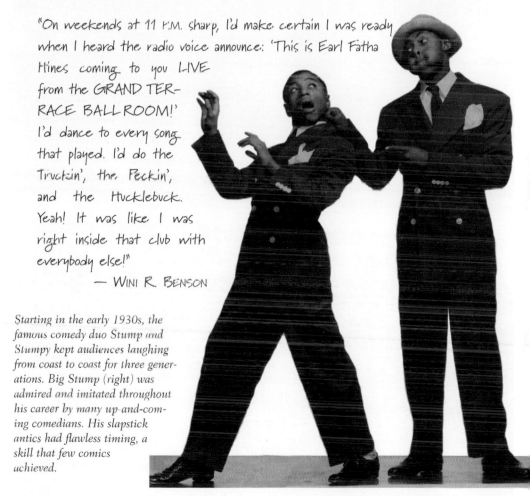

"On weekends at 11 P.M. sharp, I'd make certain I was ready when I heard the radio voice announce: 'This is Earl Fatha Hines coming to you LIVE from the GRAND TERRACE BALLROOM!' I'd dance to every song that played. I'd do the Truckin', the Peckin', and the Hucklebuck. Yeah! It was like I was right inside that club with everybody else!"
— WINI R. BENSON

Starting in the early 1930s, the famous comedy duo Stump and Stumpy kept audiences laughing from coast to coast for three generations. Big Stump (right) was admired and imitated throughout his career by many up-and-coming comedians. His slapstick antics had flawless timing, a skill that few comics achieved.

Home entertainment could also be provided by board games and, for girls, dolls. Girls took pride and joy in their dolls, but in Bronzeville the fact of the matter was that it was very difficult for African-American girls to get a doll that looked like them. Most dolls of the 1930s had pinkish-white skin, silky hair, and features that did not resemble most African-American girls.

All little girls wanted dolls that looked like the stars they flocked to see at the Saturday movie matinees, like this Shirley Temple doll from an advertisment in "Woman's World," 1936.

"Black dolls? I never thought about a Black doll. I wanted the dolls I saw in the store windows. The White ones with the long, blonde hair and the big, blue eyes. That's who I thought I looked like. Oh yeah! I even remember taking a half-slip and putting it over my head and everything that was hanging down was hair, baby! Just like my dolls."

— SWERSIE (TURPIN) NORRIS

There was one doll company that did make brown dolls. It was founded in 1918 by two Black women, Evelyn Berry and Victoria Ross. The dolls came in all sizes and styles with prices from twenty-five cents to fifteen dollars. They were called "Berry's Famous Brown Skin Dolls." These dolls appealed to White customers as well as Black ones. The dolls were sold in large department stores, mainly in New York City, Boston, Philadelphia, and a few other cities, so it was almost impossible to find one of these dolls in Chicago. By the 1920s this company,

A girl's best friend, around 1900.

78

like so many other Black-owned and -operated businesses in the early twentieth century, went out of business. But somehow enough brown dolls survived, making their way to the Midwest and to Chicago, right into the eager arms of a few lucky young girls.

"I remember getting a Black doll one Christmas. I was around twelve years old. It was 'hot stuff' having a Black doll. I had White dolls but they didn't look like me. This doll looked like me. This doll was my baby."

— GWENDOLYN KING

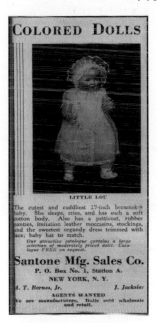

COLORED DOLLS

LITTLE LOU

The cutest and cuddliest 27-inch brownskin baby. She sleeps, cries, and has such a soft cotton body. Also has a petticoat, rubber panties, imitation leather moccasins, stockings, and the sweetest organdy dress trimmed with lace; baby hat to match.

Our attractive catalogue contains a large selection of moderately priced dolls. Catalogue FREE on request.

Santone Mfg. Sales Co.
P. O. Box No. 1, Station A.
NEW YORK, N. Y.
A. T. Barnes, Jr.   J. Jacksier
AGENTS WANTED
We are manufacturers. Dolls sold wholesale and retail.

Advertisement, 1934.

"When I moved to Chicago it was Christmas Day. I thought I was just coming for a visit, so I didn't bring my favorite doll. She was a tall Black doll, almost as tall as me. I was small for my age, you know. And I really loved that doll. We never went back to St. Louis to get our things because an uncle packed our belongings and sent them to us. Nobody told him about my doll. That's the only thing I missed about back home when we moved to Chicago. That's the only thing I missed." — ETTA LEE (MORRIS) STEPHENS

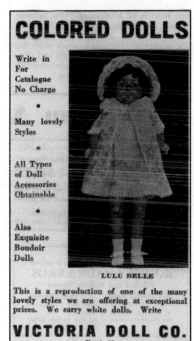

COLORED DOLLS

Write in
For
Catalogue
No Charge

•

Many lovely
Styles

•

All Types
of Doll
Accessories
Obtainable

•

Also
Exquisite
Boudoir
Dolls

LULU BELLE

This is a reproduction of one of the many lovely styles we are offering at exceptional prices. We carry white dolls. Write

VICTORIA DOLL CO.
Dept. M
18 W. 21st St.   New York City

Advertisement, 1936.

And then there were those wonderful, one-of-a-kind homemade brown cloth dolls. What a special treasure these were.

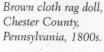

"I had a brown doll. My aunt who was from Memphis made her for me one Christmas when I was eight or nine years old. I loved that doll. She was made to look just like me. She even had two pigtails like I always wore, and my aunt made matching dresses for us too! Yes, I loved that doll. I remember taking her everywhere I'd go. To me, my doll was as real as my new baby brother Mama carried around."

—JUNE (JOHNSON) FINCH

Brown cloth rag doll, Chester County, Pennsylvania, 1800s.

It's easy to see why Hester fell in love with her new doll right from the start. There weren't many brown dolls like Minnie, and the fact that she had been made by Hester's grandmother made her that much more special.

Brown cloth rag doll brought to Chicago during her family's migration from the South, 1890s.

Cake Recipe

Make a delicious dessert just like Mama's!

Butter Pound Cake

1 *pound butter*
1 *pound powdered sugar*
3 *cups cake flour*
6 *eggs*
1 *tablespoon vanilla extract*

1. Cream butter and sugar together.

2. Sift in 1 cup of cake flour, then add 2 eggs and mix well.

3. Sift in 1 more cup of cake flour, then add 2 more eggs and mix well.

4. Sift in the remaining cup of cake flour, add the last 2 eggs, and mix well.

5. Add the vanilla extract and mix well.

6. Pour batter into a well-greased and floured bundt or tube cake pan.

7. Bake at 300° to 350° for 1 hour and 15 minutes. Before removing the cake from the oven, check to see if it is done. Insert a knife in the center of the cake. If the knife is clean when you pull it out, the cake is ready. If the knife has moist batter on it, bake the cake for an additional 15 minutes.

Recipe courtesy of Myrtle V. (Benson) Mallory, retired schoolteacher who grew up in Bronzeville, at 5740 South Calumet Avenue, during the Great Depression.

The Adventures of Minnie
Explore the Magic

Coming Soon

Minnie's Risky Rescue

Minnie is all set to enjoy the parade — but the toys have another plan for her.

Minnie's Haunted Halloween

Minnie's trick-or-treat adventure turns into a night of mystery.